This Boxer Books paperback belongs to

. . . .

www.boxerbooks.com

Reindeer

Pig

Porcupine

Toucan

Flamingo

Crocodile

Call Me Gorgeous!

Written by

Giles Milton

Illustrated by

Alexandra Milton

BOXER BOOKS

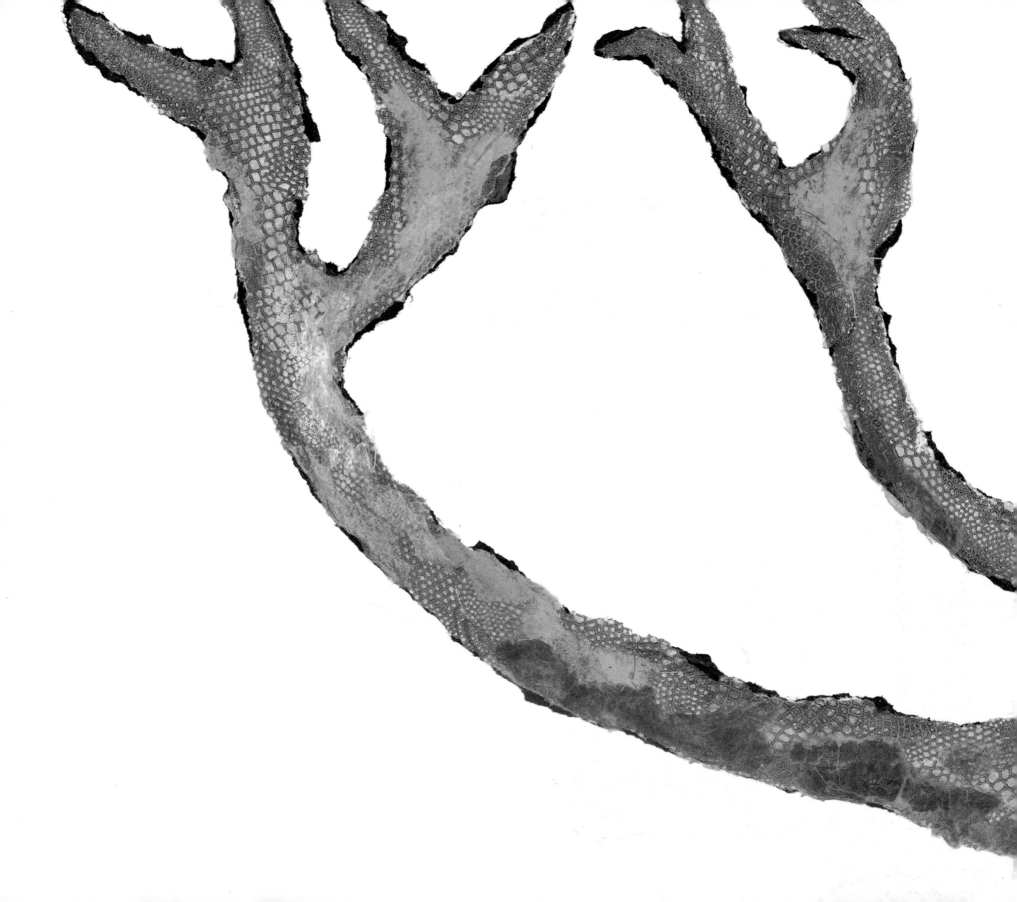

I've got
reindeer antlers

and the ears of a pig.

A porcupine's spines

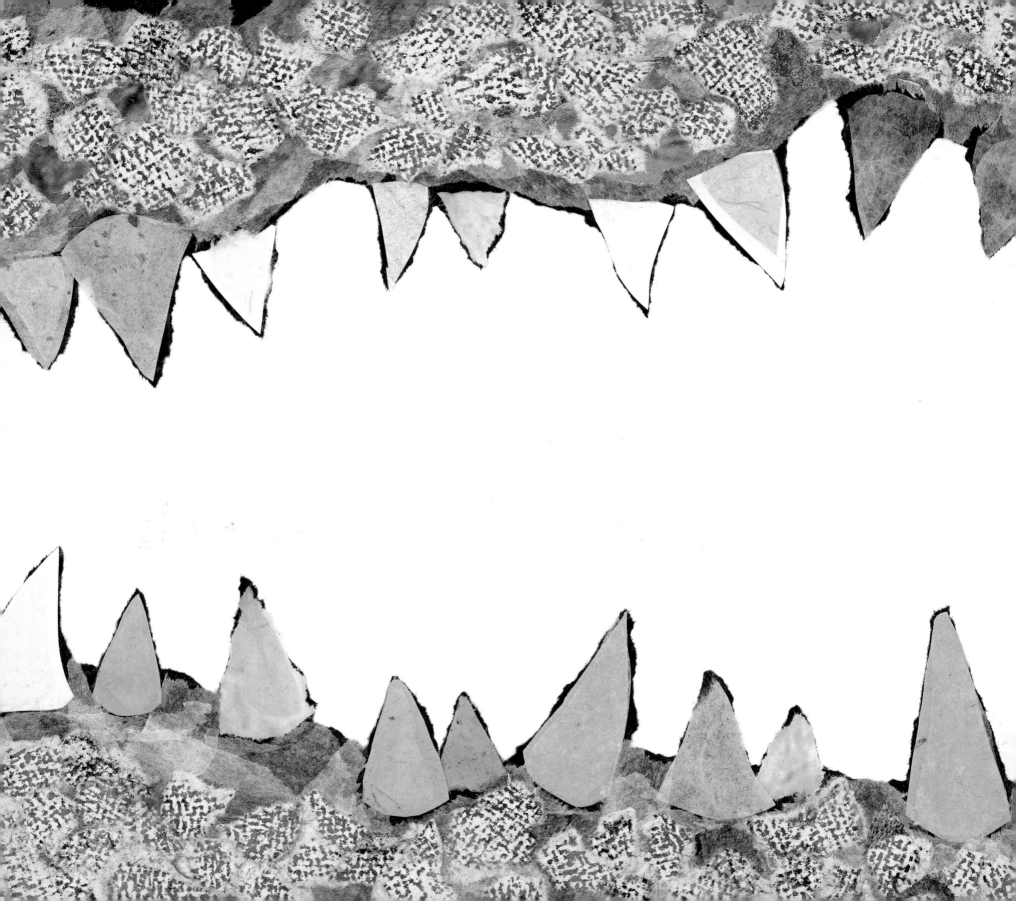

and a
crocodile's teeth.

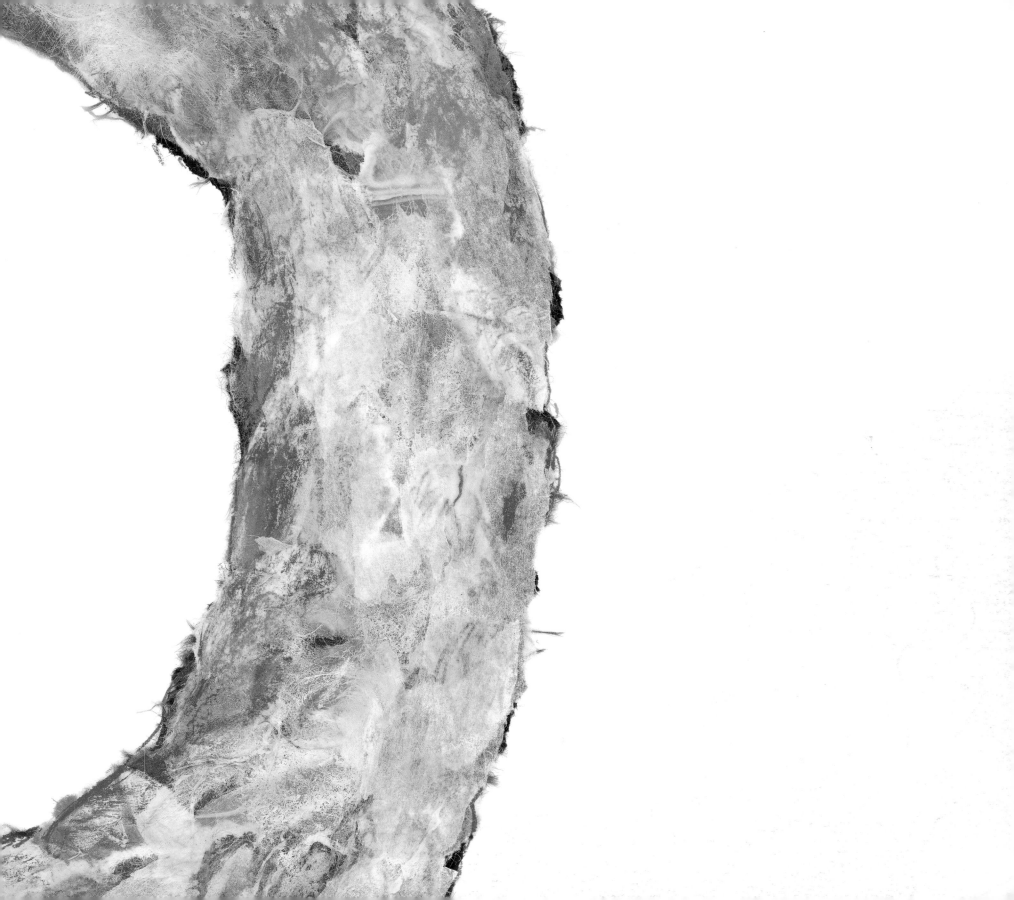

and a
cockerel's feet.

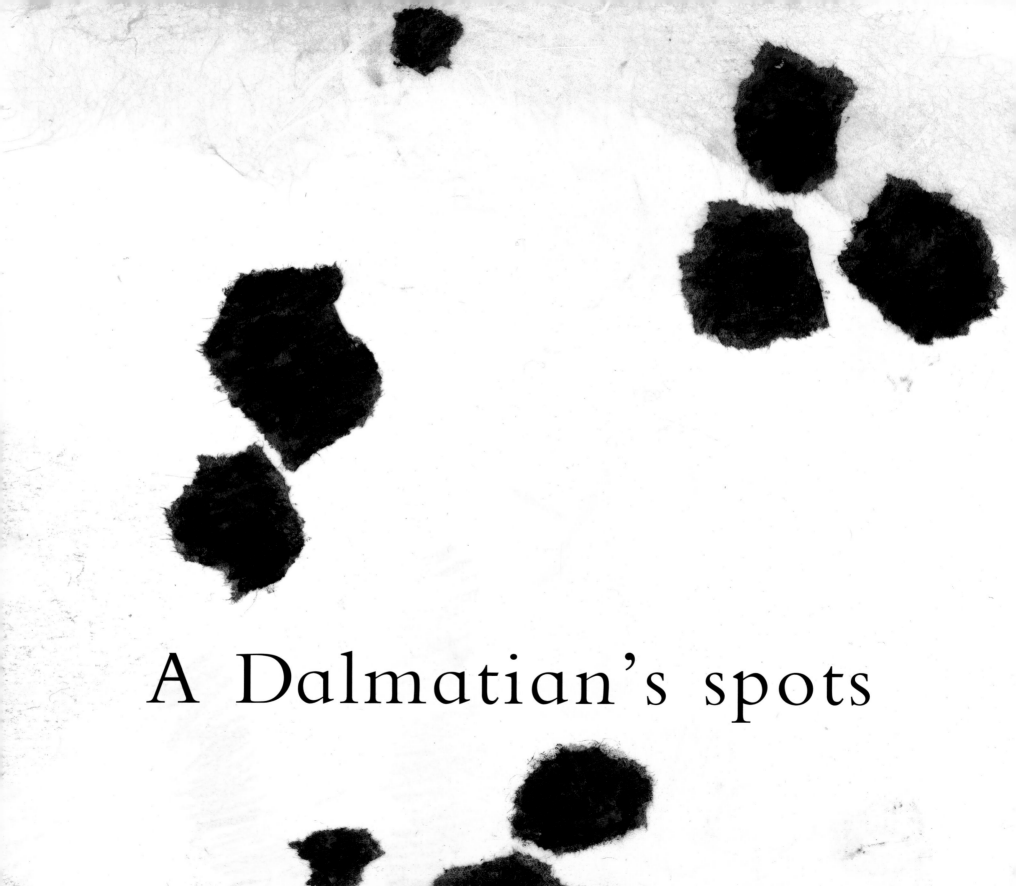

A Dalmatian's spots

and a
chameleon's tail.

The wings
of a bat

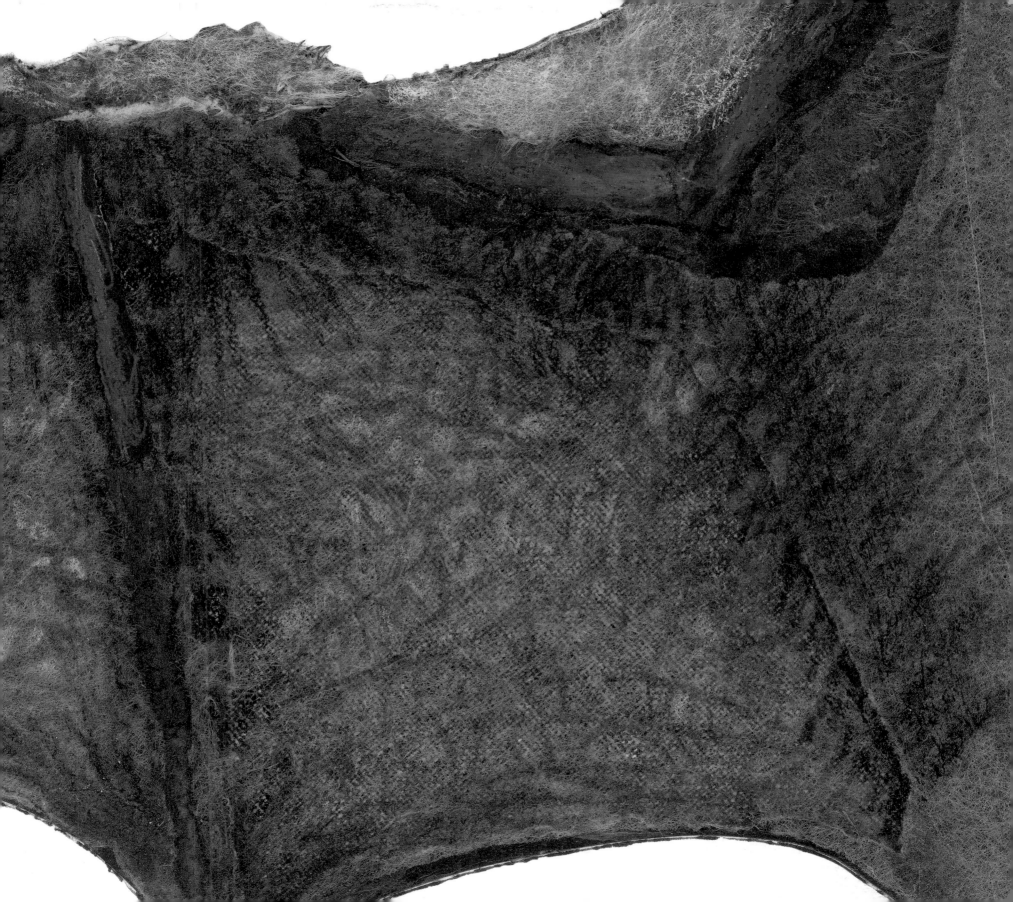

and the
eyes of a frog.

I'm a reinde-piggy-
porcu-croco-touca-
flami-cocker-
dalma-chameleo-
bat-frog.
But...

you can call me

GORGEOUS!

For Madeleine, Héloïse, Aurélia – all gorgeous.
Giles and Alexandra Milton

First published in hardback in Great Britain in 2009 by Boxer Books Limited.
First published in paperback in Great Britain in 2011 by Boxer Books Limited.
www.boxerbooks.com

The illustrations were prepared using colour pencils
and handmade paper from around the world. The text is set in Bembo Schoolbook.

ISBN 978-1-907152-49-8

1 3 5 7 9 10 8 6 4 2

Printed in China

All of our papers are sourced from managed forests and renewable resources.

Cockerel

Dalmatian

Chameleon

Bat

Frog

More Boxer Books paperbacks to enjoy

Boys Are Best! • **Manuela Olten**

A fun and irreverent story, told from the point of view of two opinionated young boys. The boys think girls are silly scaredy cats, but they turn out to be far from brave themselves when the subject of ghosts is brought up.

ISBN 978-1-905417-66-7

Chicky Chicky Chook Chook • **Cathy MacLennan**

Chicky chicks, buzzy bees and kitty cats romp in the sun and snuggle in the warmth, until pitter-patter, down comes the rain. A great read-aloud, sing-along book, full of fun-to-imitate animal sounds, rhythm and movement.

ISBN 978-1-905417-32-2

Little Smudge • **Lionel Le Néouanic**

A simple, elegant and innovative tale about the importance of mixing, making friends and appreciating differences. The illustrations cleverly incorporate shapes from well-known paintings, creating a charming tale that offers a gentle introduction to modern art.

ISBN 978-1-905417-23-0

www.boxerbooks.com